A 30–Day Devotional for Understanding the Call

Preparing to Serve In Ministry

By
Michael Pope

<u>ABOUT THE AUTHOR</u>

Michael Pope is Pastor and founder of New Life Christian Center Outreach in Birmingham, AL. He also founded, and heads Michael Pope Ministries, Inc. Michael Pope Ministries presently serves an online community of believers with a daily word of encouragement as well as weekly teachings to enhance the spiritual growth of its' followers. He is the author of two other books; *An Encouraging Word: A 30-Day Devotional* and *Encourage Yourself In The Lord*. He is a graduate of Livingston University, presently known as The University of West Alabama and Morehouse Interdenominational Theological Center. He is married to Juanita and resides in Tuscaloosa, AL.

TABLE OF CONTENTS

Introduction

Receiving God's call into ministry can be an exciting time in a person's life and leaves you with questions about what God requires of you to function in a leadership capacity. Each member in the body of Christ has a calling unique to the purpose and plan God has for their life to serve in ministry to promote the kingdom of God in the earth. With the call, there will always be a degree of uncertainty as to what I should do, where I should be, and to what people group I am called to minister. The call of God for every individual who has been called is unique, but each person is called uniquely.

Whether you have heard the voice of God internally, been the recipient of a prophetic word, been inspired through Holy Scripture, or seen visions in your dreams, as you embark on this journey, you can take comfort in the fact that your divine call will be a powerful motivator. However, the inevitable uncertainty may challenge your acceptance and execution of this call. It's a unique path driven by spiritual passion and hindered by human doubt. Most people who God calls will initially resist because many will feel unworthy of the calling, but God's divine enablement and protection will eventually cause you to respond fully.

This devotional is therefore designed to help you understand the process of the call of God so that you learn your appropriate role in this preparation for entering into the work of ministry. Carefully and prayerfully study this devotional daily and allow the Holy Spirit to minister to you and bring clarity to discovering God's assignment that He has determined for your life.

Day 1: **Live With Purpose**

"Many plans are in a man's mind, but it is the Lord's purpose for him that will stand." - Proverbs 19:21 (AMP)

Whenever I read this verse, it always pulls me back to that place in my life when I lived under a false perception: when the enemy's wiles blinded me.

"Among them, the god of this world [Satan] has blinded the minds of the unbelieving to prevent them from seeing the illuminating light of the gospel of the glory of Christ, who is the image of God." - 2 Corinthians 4:4 (AMP)

Proverbs 14:12 and Proverbs 16:25 say that there is a way that seems right to a man, BUT the end thereof is the way of death. I had so many plans in my mind about what I wanted my life to be, and looking back with the understanding of what God has taught me today, I now understand why they never worked out as planned. Although these plans, or devices as the KJV states, were good, they were not according to the purpose for which I was created. My many plans for my life did not include God but were thought out with the world's pleasures in mind. These plans had no purpose, only an inclination to fulfill my selfish desires.

What was happening throughout my life was that my plans were being overruled by the plan and purpose which God had for me. Unbeknown to me was that I had been predestined to and called to a purpose in life that would bring glory to the kingdom of God and good to my life. There was never any peace in those many plans I continued to come up with, and they were always filled with many toils, which eventually caused those plans to come to naught. Things just wouldn't work out with any sustaining power. They would start well but soon come to an end.

This was all because only what we do for Christ will stand. Our course has already been set, and we await our discovery so that we run it and fulfill our chosen purpose in life. That is why the enemy works so hard to keep us from hearing the words of the Lord. He seeks to keep us in the dark, pushing us to exclude the Lord from our lives and preventing us from hearing His guidance. Yet, the Lord counters these efforts by provoking us to question the reasons behind our choices, thus thwarting such plans.

Once we are enlightened and sanctified in the truth, the Word of God (John 17:17), His counsel begins to speak to our conscience and softens our hearts so that we begin to understand and see life from His perspective. Then we realize that we were created with a purpose in life beyond our selfish ambitions. The struggles you experienced in that life that seemed right for so many years begin to weary your conscience and cause you to look for a better way of life which we only find in Him when we turn our faces to Him. In Him, we discover our purpose in life and set our face toward fulfilling it. Once we do this, we have now begun to Live With Purpose.

*Lord, thank You for revealing my
purpose and teaching me how to walk
according to the plan You have for me. I
pray today that You will open the eyes of
my understanding as You fill me with the*

knowledge of Your will so that all that I do will be pleasing in Your sight. In Jesus' Name, I Pray, Amen.

Day 2: **The Cost For The Journey**

"So likewise, whosoever he be of you that forsakes not all that he hath, he cannot be My disciple." - Luke 14:33 (NKJV)

While we were all born with a purpose in life, we all have different assignments to spread the gospel message to the lost. To be effective and fulfill your purpose in life requires that we all go through stages of development to be adequately prepared to do the work given to us. Jesus left us with words of comfort:

I have told you these things so that in Me you may have [perfect] peace. In the world, you have tribulation and distress and suffering, but be courageous [be confident, be undaunted, be filled with joy]; I have overcome the world." - John 16:33 (AMP)

He informed us that we would have tribulations in this world once we decide to follow Him, but He assures us that He has already deprived them of any power to harm us. Often we will see those who receive their salvation and immediately are on fire for the Lord. They are excited and want to save the world by sharing this wonderful thing God has just done in their life. I'd like to say that these individuals, in their zeal, have not had enough time to grasp or understand Jesus's words about the spiritual warfare that every believer will have to engage in. So many good intentions never come to fruition because we never know there will be challenges with every good intention.

I heard this saying one day that shed light on things happening in my life once I started this ministry. He said that the greater the assignment, the greater the level of development required. These words of wisdom gave me a clear understanding of the attacks constantly coming against me in a season. Truthfully, when I was given this assignment, I thought things would happen in a reasonable amount of time and without all the hardships. But I have learned that a greater level of development does not develop when things are well, but rather it is in those valley experiences where we learn to trust God and grow in our faith into mature Christians who have yielded to the guidance of the Holy Spirit.

There is a cost for this journey that we must take account of. There will be sacrifices that will have to be made if we desire to move forward.

The enthusiasm I previously held for football, which consumed my weekends with both college and professional matches, has now been supplanted. This commitment has transitioned towards a dedication to studying God's Word. My energy is now channeled into preparing weekly lessons and personal discipline, shaping a spiritual path for my future. When I would have loved to sit down to a movie, I must utilize my time for daily bible reading and studies. The luxury of what I once called sleeping in has turned into an early rising to be alone with God in the quiet before the house, with all its distractions, comes alive. The cost of this journey is a life of self-denial and watchfulness with a constant course of holy duties. All those things that were dear to you will be lost for the sake of preparation and development to be effective and efficient in your assigned purpose.

Jesus asks the question in Luke 14:28 (AMP), "For which one of you, when he wants to build a watchtower [for his guards], does not first sit down and calculate the cost, to see if he has enough to finish it?"

We, too, must understand that there is a cost for the anointing required to do great work for the Lord, but God will provide us with all that we need to follow Him and be His disciple if we are willing to pay the cost that this journey will require. Remember the words in 2 Timothy 3:12 (AMP):

"Indeed, all who delight in pursuing righteousness and are determined to live godly lives in Christ Jesus will be hunted and persecuted [because of their faith]."

We must be willing to endure hardness as good soldiers of Jesus Christ and fight this good fight of faith regardless of the cost because your reward will be great in heaven.

Lord, thank You for the price You
paid to save me from my sins and restore
me to a right relationship with You. Since
You counted the cost and still came as a
sacrifice for me, I am willing to pay the
price to represent You here on the earth.
And thank You for the grace You provide
those willing to endure this hardness for
the sake of the Kingdom. Amen.

Day 3: **New Level New Devil**

"Because a wide door for effective service has opened to me [in Ephesus, a very promising opportunity], and there are many adversaries." - 1 Corinthians 16:9 (AMP)

It was such a blessing one Sunday morning to hear a message from my Pastor on the saints not giving up during our growing season.

"Let us not grow weary or become discouraged in doing good, for at the proper time we will reap if we do not give in." - Galatians 6:9 (AMP)

He touched on seedtime and harvest from Genesis 8:22 to tell us that growth happens before the reaping but during the growing season, not to give up. We are not to grow weary and faint during this time. Then, he closed out the message by sharing that during our growing season, there will be different levels of anointing to get us to our destiny.

So, one morning as I was going over my notes from his message, God spoke to me and said that at every level we reach, there would be a new devil there attempting to thwart God's plan and purpose that God has for your life. He said that the greater the calling, the harder the enemy will fight to prevent you from reaching your destiny.

At every level you reach, a new devil will be waiting to oppose the work God is doing in you. He will try to sway you away from the path you are now on with fear and doubt. He will send new temptations you have never had to face before. Distractions will begin to surface from every direction.

Don't be mistaken; the fighting becomes more intense at every level. When you make it to your stay in the boat level of receiving your salvation, the devil only needs to try and steal from you what you didn't understand in your infancy stage. But, as you begin to grow and seek a more intimate relationship, which begins to spark a desire to do more work promoting the Kingdom of God, the big boys start to come after you. The enemy won't roll out the red carpet for you but will fight you tooth and nail to prevent you from reaching your place of destination. Think about James:

"Consider it nothing but joy, my [a]brothers and sisters, whenever you fall into various trials. Be assured that the testing of your faith [through experience] produces endurance [leading to spiritual maturity, and inner peace]."
– James 1:2-3 (AMP)

These verses tell us to count it all joy when faced with these various temptations. A child of God can have joy in the midst of adversities because of what he knows. Regardless of what we have to face, God has already girded us with the strength to withstand the attack because this battle is not our own, but it belongs to the Lord, Who will fight for us if we just hold our peace, stand our ground, and not give up in our well doing. Just a word of warning as you move ahead in the things of God from faith to faith and from glory to glory; at every level you reach, there will be a new devil to fight, but remember, WE ALWAYS WIN!

Father, thank You for Your sufficient
grace and new mercies You provide me
every day so that I can continue to fight
this good fight of faith, not in my own

*strength, but by the empowerment I
receive through my union with You to
fight each new devil at every level that
You bring me into. In Jesus' Name. Amen.*

Day 4: **Up Is Actually Down**

"Humble yourselves in the sight of the Lord, and He will lift you up." - James 4:10 (NKJV)

While sitting in a meeting where we were discussing being diligent in making our calling and election sure:

"Therefore, brethren, be even more diligent to make your call and election sure, for if you do these things, you will never stumble;" - 2 Peter 1:10 (NKJV)

I was reminded of the words I heard in a sermon some time ago about how we are to reach that place of our calling, which God has predestined us to be. Simply put, the way up is always down first. It has become clear that God has to strip us of our pride and self-sufficiency before surrendering to His will for our life. We were not born with a desire to seek God and His way of life, but it was the total opposite:

"There is none who understands; There is none who seeks after God." - Romans 3:11 (NKJV)

Therefore, throughout our life, before we acknowledged and accepted God, we built a dependency on doing our things our way. Then, we accepted Jesus into our hearts, and now for us to be fit for the Master's use and elevated to that appointed place of our calling, God has to strip us of SELF. We now must learn how to lay down our will and seek God's will every day of our born-again life.

After years of being the captain of our own ship, God has to peel off SELF layer by layer until we experience our Gethsemane and cry out, "Not my will Lord, but Your will be done." It's usually the mental hardship we experience when the Holy Spirit and the Word of God dissect us because of the opposition we put up in our minds that causes us to make wrong decisions and actions, knocking us down. We don't always understand the ordering of our steps which the Lord is doing because it usually contradicts our preconceived idea of what direction and way we should take.

It is not always easy for one to accept that he didn't have it all together as he thought, nor that his way is not the way that God has chosen for him. God wants to elevate His chosen to levels where we will be most effective in furthering the Kingdom, but first, He must rid us of the biggest hindrance to the work He desires to do in us, which is SELF. True humility is when you have set aside your will to do the will of God.

Before I came to the place of accepting God's will for my life, I could not understand the adversity I was constantly facing. These things caused me to come after God with an enthusiasm I never had before. He revealed that I needed to be free of SELF before He could elevate me, and the way up is down first. There has been stripping, losses, hurt, and pain to knock me down from the place of SELF so that my total dependency is now on Him. Every crutch that I was not aware of and leaning on has been removed. Now when I look at the place I am in Him today, Him speaking to me about my future while I'm in this lowly place of my transformation, I now understand the way Up Is Actually Down first.

Father, today I want to thank You for
the work that You have begun in me to

transform me into the person You created me to be so that I fulfill my calling in life according to Your purpose. Teach me how to acknowledge You in all my ways as I accept the direction You desire to take me so that I am most effective in my calling. Amen.

Day 5: **In Transition**

"For this reason, we also, since the day we heard it, do not cease to pray for you, and to ask that you may be filled with the knowledge of His will in all wisdom and spiritual understanding;" - Colossians 1:9 (NKJV)

When we speak of transition, let it be clear that we are not referring to a geographical move but rather a spiritual repositioning that moves us to a greater level of anointing for a greater work of ministry. As we open ourselves to the will of God and accept the assignment He has for us, it requires a spiritual education for increased knowledge of Him and His ways. This is where God sharpens our spiritual awareness so that our perspective changes and we become aware of what is required to move us from one level to the next.

Transition can be very uncomfortable for an individual as he will always face uncertainties. Here, you must develop a level of trust, for the path that leads to your place will always be clouded by a lack of understanding. Things happen during your transition, preparing you to better serve in your place that doesn't make much sense to the finite mind. But as you travel this path by faith one step at a time, it eventually becomes clearer, but it still can be uncomfortable.

Embarking on an unfamiliar path is inevitably fraught with uncertainty, clouding our understanding of our destination. Yet, through such transitions, our faith is most intensely engaged. God, in His divine plan, seeks to elevate you to a heightened state of anointing, where your purpose finds its fullest expression. To facilitate this journey, He diligently works to remove the extraneous elements in your life, purging you of all that is unneeded in your designated place.

As you navigate through transitions, you learn to trust God's plan for your life. By doing so, you permit Him to guide your steps, ensuring your arrival at your designated place of service and your readiness for it. The journey of transition itself equips and prepares you, refining your abilities for the responsibilities that lie ahead.

Those yokes meant to keep you bound are destroyed in transition, the burdens are lifted, and everything hindering your service in your assigned place will be stripped. Transition moves you from an elementary level of faith to a faith that develops into that trust of whatever He desires for your life, then let it be done. Job couldn't understand what was happening to his life, yet he stated, "Though He slays me, yet will I trust Him" (Job 13:15).

Not that God does anything to harm His own, but Job made it clear that he trusted God regardless of how painful his path had turned. So it is in our spiritual transition; it is uncomfortable to move from what may have been a comfortable position for us to move into another area or arena that causes uncertainties as we make this shift. But as we go, our faith has to move to that level of trust so that, as Job, we go where He leads, regardless of how painful the journey may be.

Father, thank You that although the
transition can be uncomfortable, You are

always there with me to comfort me along the way. I pray for strength and courage as You lead me along this path. Give me the grace to accept Your plan for my life and the process required to transition me to my assigned place of service. Amen!

Day 6: **In This Season**

"But as for me, I trust in You, O Lord; I say, "You are my God." My times are in Your hand; Deliver me from the hand of my enemies," – Psalm 31:14 - 15 (NKJV)

Getting to the place God has shown you in the spirit requires you first to be content with your present season. To faithfully persevere in this walk of faith and reach your destiny depends on seeing every situation and circumstance from God's perspective. In this season of your life, God is preparing and rearranging things so that you will arrive at your destiny in time and with every provision you need available and in place.

During this pivotal season, God is meticulously pruning away those elements and individuals not integral to His divine plan for your life. Maintaining a steadfast focus on Jesus is paramount now more than ever as you transition to a higher level of consecration. It is essential to purify yourself, to prepare for stepping into your destined place, unburdened by anything that may taint the sanctity of where God is guiding you.

In Joshua 5:8 (NKJV), the text says, "So it was when they had finished circumcising all the people, that they stayed in their places in the camp till they were healed."

That's why God is hiding you right now. There doesn't seem to be any connections; you are not drawn to others now, and something is stirring within that you have no point of reference for, nor can you explain. You just appear to be in a place or space where you only want to experience more of

God's presence in your life. In what seems like isolation to you, God is using this season to heal you of all your past wounds and pain before you enter this place.

You cannot be effective in your ministry until you have been delivered from your flesh; therefore, He is using this time to cut away all those old tendencies, habits, and dependencies which will hinder the work God has for you. As our text explains, the key to this season is that you trust God. You must be willing to give the Lord control of every aspect of your life. You will understand that your time is in his hands when you do. The word 'times' is translated as "season, or due season."

This is where contentment plays its part. You must be satisfied with the season you are in while God is taking you to that place He has revealed to you in your spirit. A right perspective of what God is doing allows you to accept where you are now and won't allow you to grow weary as the process unfolds one step at a time. Proverbs 4:18 says, "…the path of the just is as the shining light, that shines more and more (brighter and clearer) unto the perfect day."

Just keep walking by faith and know that In This Season, God is perfecting everything which concerns you so that you are adequately prepared to walk into your destiny and function at the level intended to bring glory to His Kingdom. Be steadfast and unmovable by standing your ground, understanding that your times are in God's hands.

Father, thank You for the work You
are doing in me In This Season to prepare
me to walk into my destiny and bring

*glory and honor to Your name. I pray that
patience has its' perfect work in me so
that contentment covers me as a shield.
Amen.*

Day 7: **Courage To Walk With God**

"Have I not commanded you? Be strong and of good courage; do not be afraid, nor be dismayed, for the Lord your God is with you wherever you go." - Joshua 1:9 (KJV)

If anyone ever told you that walking with God is easy, they misled you. It takes focus, determination, and energy to walk with God. Walking with God denotes not getting ahead of Him, so waiting becomes one of the most difficult disciplines Christians are called to practice. We stress walking with God because many don't dare to wait on God, creating an over-eagerness to act on your own without receiving clear divine instructions. Trusting God and walking with Him in His strength and timing takes courage.

Courage is needed to do it God's way and not your own. The faint in heart will usually step out ahead of God because of the fear of missing Him when they have perceived with their intellect what they think is the right time to move or what God desires for them to do. Courage is the ability to do something that frightens you. One thing you can be assured of is this; when God asks something of you, it's usually something you cannot do in your own strength. So to walk with Him will require courage.

"In conclusion, be strong in the Lord [draw your strength from Him and be empowered through your union with Him] and in the power of His [boundless] might." - Ephesians 6:10 (AMP)

This verse gives instructions on how to walk out the plan and purpose of God for your life. He tells us to "be strong in the Lord [be empowered through your union with Him]; draw your strength from Him [that strength which His boundless might provides]." God knew that the fear of the unknown may have gripped Joshua's heart, so He commanded him to "be strong and of good courage."

God told him, 'what I am asking you to do is beyond your ability, but I'm giving you a command to have courage.' Sometimes we have to do what God wants even when we are afraid; therefore, you need courage to walk with Him knowing that regardless of what He asks of you, He said He would be with you to accomplish His plan. He told Joshua to be strong and of good courage, to not be afraid, nor to be dismayed. To be dismayed means to be terrified and discouraged, which will eventually cause you to break down.

When we don't see the provision needed to accomplish what God has asked of us, we tend to allow the fear of the unknown to terrify us and prevent us from moving ahead. But you will need the courage to walk with God without a doubt. It takes a boldness that comes only from Him to walk out the plan He has for your life. You will need courage to withstand the attacks and stand on what God has spoken to you.

"For the Spirit God gave us does not make us timid, but gives us power, love and self-discipline." – 2 Timothy 1:7 (NIV)

The verse mentioned above urges you to understand that fear will always show its face to try and prevent you from stepping out on what God has spoken to you. If you don't check fear at the door, you will allow a spirit of fear to come in, eventually paralyzing you and preventing you from moving forward. So, walking with God means you do just that, and you move even if you have to do it, afraid, knowing that God is with you and that your strength comes from Him because you have been commanded to "be strong and of good courage."

Father, thank You for the strength
You provide in my times of weakness.
Teach me daily how to walk in a holy
boldness that allows me to fulfill Your
will. In Jesus' Name, I Pray, Amen.

Day 8: **In God's Timing**

"Listen to counsel and receive instruction, That you may be wise in your latter days. There are many plans in a man's heart. Nevertheless, the Lord's counsel—that will stand." - Proverbs 19: 20 – 21 NKJV)

When we take into account the life of Jesus in the book of Luke, we see Jesus in the temple at twelve years of age, sitting down with the teachers of the Law, hearing and asking questions (Luke 3:46). Then, over in Luke 4:18, some eighteen years later again, we see Him in the synagogue reading from the book of Isaiah declaring to them that this scripture of Isaiah 61:1-3 which He was reading is fulfilled in Him.

This was the start of His earthly ministry, which began when He was now thirty years old (Luke 3:21-23). Although He stripped Himself of His divinity when He came to earth as a man, He was still fully God and had to wait until the Father determined the time to start His earthly ministry. Luke 2:40 says of Him that "the child grew, and waxed strong in spirit, filled with wisdom: and the grace of God was upon Him." Then Luke 3:52 states, "And Jesus increased in wisdom and stature, and in favor with God."

I conclude here that everything was done in God's timing. Today we are seeing people who may have received a call from God deciding for themselves when their time to step out has come. Although no one can question someone's calling, some evidence or fruit should be visible. If the Son of God, Jesus Christ himself, had to wait before He stepped out into His calling, why do we suppose that we can decide for ourselves when it is our time to step into what God has called us to?

A calling from God does not mean that it's instantaneous. There is a waiting period, or a pruning season, in which God will strip us of ourselves so that we can allow Him to live and do a work through us. The forty years Moses spent on the backside of the mountain was used as a pruning season so that the world (his upbringing in Pharaoh's house) could be stripped out of him. The apostle Paul returned to Arabia for three years, his desert or wilderness, where he was prepared for ministry (Galatians 1:17).

People are setting their own time and saying that they have been sitting too long and are wasting away when it is actually a period of time that God is using to prepare them for the work He has called them to do. Also, the bible is very clear in instructing us not to move a novice too soon, lest they be lifted with pride when not adequately prepared. It all boils down to God's timing. Whether it is that we are zealous or maybe rebellious, we can't decide when the time for our work is to begin. Only God knows the time. We must accept this season of preparation and pruning to be most effective when God opens the door of opportunity for us.

In God's timing, He will humble you, reveal to you your purpose, and check to see what is in your heart. He has to kill the old man in your wilderness so that the new man may shine and bring Him glory. We must be willing to wait on God's Timing.

Father, I thank You for building in
me the patience to trust You as I go

through my season of preparation. Thank You for choosing me to be Your workmanship that will be fit and meet for Your use when You determine my time has come. In Jesus' Name, I Pray, Amen.

Day 9: **Wait On God's Timing**

"Counsel in the heart of man is like deep water, but a man of understanding will draw it out." - Proverbs 20:5 (NKJV)

One thing you can be sure of is God prepares His saints for the direction He will take them in life. There will always be decisions we must make if we are to walk in the plan and purpose of God. But the key is learning to wait when facing a difficult or major decision. Through diligent time in prayer and bible study, God has instilled within every believer the necessary wisdom of God to give us the ability to discern which path we must take to walk in line with His will for our life.

The patience to wait on God's timing will allow the various facets of life to fall in place and open for us when we learn to draw from the counsel of God which we have within. Our text explains this condition of every believer who has had the eyes of their understanding enlightened to the purpose and plan of God. He says that this counsel of God is available to us but is like water down in a deep well, and if we are to move in the will of God, we must rely on His voice and wisdom and not on our flesh or the wisdom of men.

The problem or key is in learning to wait. Everyone will have an opinion or think they know what is best for you, but whatever God has given you to do, the wisdom of God and His might are what you need to move forward. Waiting does require courage because there will always be pressure to act, but you must be willing to remain in your current position until you receive clear divine direction from God, not the voice of men.

If you are not careful, you might stop listening to the Lord and follow other advice. Understand that everyone is entitled to make whatever decision God leads them to without owing anyone an explanation for your decision. Don't ever allow other people to persuade you to move; rather, draw the counsel you need from the well of wisdom that God has placed within you.

Sometimes people can be so eager to help, want to draw you into their plan, or just think they can decide for others and cause you to miss what God is saying to you by their interference. The most important thing for any believer is to have his own personal relationship with God and trust that He will speak to you and give the guidance and direction you need to fulfill the purpose and plan He has for you.

One of the scriptures God gave to me during this season of preparation is "Be still and know that I am God…" (Psalm 46:10 KJV), and believe me, there has been a fight to keep the voices of others out of my head so that I can be still and allow God to work out His plan in my life. The word "still" means to make somebody or cause somebody to become quiet, calm, and undisturbed. When we get ourselves into this position of rest and are still, this is how we can draw from the well of godly counsel we have within. God has a specific purpose and plans for your life, and His timing is perfect; just be patient and trust in Him.

Father, thank You for the patience
You have instilled in me to wait on Your

*perfect timing. Continue to strengthen me
as I learn to lean on You and trust You in
all my ways. Thank You for Your wisdom
and might to move when You speak.
Amen.*

Day 10: **Requirements Of Waiting**

"Trust in the Lord with all thine heart: and lean not unto thine own understanding. In all thy ways acknowledge Him, and He will direct thy paths." - Proverbs 3:5-6 (KJV)

Waiting for God's timing is neither passive nor idle; it takes discipline and commitment. When we look deeply into our text, we see that when we say we have moved beyond the elementary level of faith to trust God, we are saying that we have accepted the truth that His ways are nothing like ours and that we are willing to wait and allow Him to direct our every step on this journey of life to reach our place of destiny.

From a human standpoint, He usually does things differently than we expect in our finite thinking, but when you have moved to the place of trusting Him, therefore learning to live in harmony with His plan, then His timing starts to make sense. Along with faith, waiting on the Lord requires humility. To wait for the Lord, you must be convinced of your need for Him – you cannot charge ahead with your plans and at the same time be fully surrendered to Him.

Humility will cause you to set aside your plans so that you discover and walk in His divine will for your life. Realizing that we are not sufficient to navigate this course of faith on our own will open us to His sovereignty and omniscience. The all-sufficient and all-knowing God knows how to get us to the place He desires when we surrender to His plan for our life.

Next, there is patience. We must be willing to remain in our current position until we receive clear divine direction. How often do we plunge ahead in things without taking the time to patiently wait on the Lord? Being zealous in our desire to serve and exercise our gifts without clear direction will lead us into things that may not have been a part of God's plan. Nevertheless, He will, and always does, take everything and use it for our good to ensure His plans are fulfilled. Waiting upon the Lord must be a deliberate decision that requires us to exercise patience. We cannot rely on fleshly emotions or the wisdom of men, but we must patiently rely on the voice of God and His wisdom.

Lastly, waiting for God requires courage, especially when there is pressure to act. Here, we must be very careful so that we don't stop listening to God and start to follow other advice. We must keep our ears attuned to the voice of Almighty God, and then we won't go wrong. Courage is needed for the decisions you will face on this journey. There will always be opportunities presented, but you must ask yourself that all-important question; is this of God, or is this me wanting to fulfill my desires?

Waiting upon the Lord is one of the wisest and most important decisions we make in life. And contrary to popular assumptions, it is an active endeavor that requires faith, humility, patience, and courage. When you rely on God and wait for His timing, you can be assured that He will guide you into that expected end He has chosen for you.

Father, I pray today that you will
open the eyes of my understanding to
Your will, purpose and plan that You have

for my life. Order my every step according to Your Word and let it illuminate the path You set before me. In Jesus' Name, Amen.

Day 11: **The Key To Waiting**

"Let your conduct be without covetousness; be content with such things as you have. For He Himself has said, 'I will never leave you nor forsake you.'" - Hebrews 13:5 (NKJV)

God has a plan and purpose for our life; the course has already been mapped out and is working according to His timing. When we avail ourselves of this truth, we must understand that when we rely upon God and wait for His timing, everything needed to prepare and equip us for our assignment will fall into place.

An important concept or principle we must first develop is trust. We must trust God to wait on Him. We never want to get ahead of God and His plans for our life. To "wait" means "to look for", "hope", and "to trust in." Proverbs 3:5 says that we are to trust the Lord with all our heart and not lean to our understanding as the path God has chosen unfolds step by step.

As important as it is for a believer to trust God, the real key to waiting is to be content right where you are. We must be satisfied with our present circumstances if we trust God to do all He has promised. How often do we become impatient with God's timing and want to move ahead of Him?

Contentment means I'm satisfied, and being content will cause you to rest because you trust God to work His will and good pleasure in your life according to His set timing. You cannot charge ahead with your plans and be fully surrendered to God simultaneously. Waiting on God requires me to be content in my present state, knowing that God is preparing me and the place of my calling so that I will function effectively in His chosen assignment.

The place that you are in right now, and whatever it is that you presently have or may be experiencing, is what God has ordered for this season of your life, and when you are content with your current state, waiting becomes a blessing because now you have accepted that our Sovereign God is working everything together for your good and His glory. So be content with such things as you have currently, and know that God will bring you to your expected end when you wait patiently on Him.

*Father, thank You for leading and
guiding me along the path which You
have chosen for me to walk, and give me
the courage and strength to patiently wait
on You being satisfied where I am now
while You take me to where I must go to
fulfill my purpose. Amen.*

Day 12: **How Are You Waiting?**

"And so, after he had patiently endured, he obtained the promise." - Hebrews 6:15 (NKJV)

Have you ever got up to begin your day, and Satan launched an all-out "what is the use" thought in your thinking?

It should come as no surprise to any believer that first thing in the morning, in your mind, the enemy will send a contradiction against what you believe to get your day started on the wrong path. Together, in our daily time of fellowship here, we have been taught to immediately cast down these negative thoughts by speaking the Word of God against them and with the <u>spoken</u> Word bringing every contrary thought into the obedience of Christ.

"casting down arguments and every high thing that exalts itself against the knowledge of God, bringing every thought into captivity to the obedience of Christ," – 2 Corinthians 10:5 (NKJV)

When you have accepted God's Word as truth and yielded to the Holy Spirit's promptings and guidance, these challenging times should not move you off the path God has placed you on. As born-again believers, we can always expect the enemy to craftily try to deceive us into agreeing with him and doubt God and His Word. So, with this attack against your thoughts, the Holy Spirit will always want to know how you are waiting for the manifestation of what He has spoken to you. Are you fretting, murmuring, and complaining, or are you patiently waiting for God to manifest the answers to your prayers?

The Amplified version of this scripture says that Abraham waited long and endured patiently, then realized and obtained what God had promised him. We, too, must endure every hardship, trial, and challenge in this walk of faith with patience that says we trust God to do all He has promised He would do in our life. When everything else around us may be like sinking sand, we must patiently stand on our Rock, knowing He is faithful to do all He has promised.

We do not fret because we see the fruition of other people's blessings. We do not murmur about how long we have waited, nor do we complain when we get a little weary during our waiting time. But with patience, we enter that place of rest and wait as God works all things together for our good so that His plan is fulfilled.

Regardless of how things may look or what you feel, patiently endure all to receive the blessings promised to you. Keep rejoicing about what you know God will do in your life by believing and agreeing with God's Word. And most importantly, in everything, no matter the circumstance, be thankful and always thank God.

"in everything give thanks; for this is the will of God in Christ Jesus for you." - 1 Thessalonians 5:18 (NKJV)

With all that we believers must face in this life of faith, the question for you today is, How Are You Waiting?

Father, thank You for the peace You have given me within to wait with a patient expectation of what we know You will do. Today I pray for the strength in my heart to keep my focus on You and Your Word and maintain a joyful attitude as I wait. In Jesus' Name, I Pray, Amen.

Day 13: **Courage To Move**

"And the Lord, He it is that doth go before thee; He will be with thee, He will not fail thee, neither forsake thee: fear not, neither be dismayed." - Deuteronomy 31:8 (KJV)

Often when we cry out for direction and guidance, it may be possible that we are experiencing some reservations or even fear of the unknown ahead of us. Although this path can sometimes be dark and confusing, we are called to move forward into the unknown armed only with trust in God. It can be difficult and unsettling to move forward with the lamp of God's guidance shining only a step or two ahead of us. Before we move, we want to know more, we want to see what lies ahead, and we want a guarantee of success. We want to be sure that we are traveling the path God has chosen for us rather than one in which we seek to fulfill our selfish desires and ambition.

Therefore, we seek prayer for guidance and direction when the truth comes. We may be nursing our worries and fears of the unknown because by spending quality time alone with the Word and God in prayer, the path He has chosen may have already been laid out before us. In His presence, He will instruct and teach us the way He has chosen for us, and we will discover that He has ordered our every step to align with the path He has chosen for us to follow.

"The steps of a [good and righteous] man are directed and established by the Lord, And He delights in his way [and blesses his path]." - Psalm 37:23 (AMP)

I pose the question then; are we unsure of the path God has for us, or do we lack the courage and confidence to move forward? So as we see God instructing Joshua to move forward, He commands him to be strong and courageous and not to allow any fearful thoughts or worries to enter his thinking.

"Have I not commanded you? Be strong and of good courage; do not be afraid, nor be dismayed, for the Lord your God is with you wherever you go." – Joshua 1:9 (NKJV)

First, it takes courage to trust God, and then we must be strong and courageous to move forward into the unknown at God's command. We were all called out of the kingdom of darkness, translated into the kingdom of His Son, and commissioned to work for the Kingdom. So, there is a path that God has chosen for each of us to walk so that His purposes are fulfilled in our lives, and yes, it requires courage to step out into the unknown.

As you ponder the thought of God's plan for your life, and come seeking guidance and direction, remember that God has commanded you to be courageous and to walk in the way which He lays out before you because His eye of guidance is upon you to lead you on the path He has chosen.

*Father, thank You for strengthening
me in my inner man and giving me the
courage to walk the path You have
chosen for my life. Grant me the
understanding and wisdom to accept all
You have chosen for me. In Jesus' Name,
Amen.*

Day 14: **When Do I Move**

"And it happened after a while that the brook dried up, because there had been no rain in the land." - 1 Kings 17:7 (NKJV)

As we travel on this life journey and have committed to trusting God to lead and direct our path, we must discern when God is telling us to move. This is an area in which we sometimes will stay in one place too long because we may have become comfortable in our surroundings or become so close to others that we fail to understand when God is stirring the nest to move us forward to our chosen place of destiny. A very profound truth supports this; "relationships and friendships corrupt principles."

Once you have gotten all that you can get out of the place where you are presently, God may be telling you that in this season of your journey that this place has become dry and barren for you because it is time to move to a place of the new provision He has prepared for you. Just as the prophet Elijah had experienced this provision which caused him to mature in his faith as he followed the command of God and went to the place which he had been commanded to go, we too will have to follow the voice of God to get into the place of His choosing for Him to sustain us while He equips and prepares us for the next phase of our journey.

But the brook will dry up when you have received all God can give you in a particular place. It will lose the refreshing, revitalizing nourishment it once provided you and become dry. There won't be the hunger and thirst you once possessed because you may have outgrown your surroundings and now need to be thrust forward so that you seek higher levels so that you fulfill and walk in the spiritual realm God preordained for you to operate in.

God led Elijah to Zarephath, where faith is tested, and the improbable becomes possible. We, too, must understand that when God allows the brook from which you were once fed to dry up, it may be the time for you to move on. Then, when you step out on your faith and get into the right place, that is the place where you will begin to see the manifestation of God's provision for your life.

Don't neglect to take that step of faith because of fear and doubt, but be very clear that if God has dried up the brook that once nourished you, it is a sign that you are now ready to move to another place of provision and experience God in a completely different way.

Father, thank You for the promptings
of Your Holy Spirit, Who is my Helper
that will lead me into all truth and give
me peace when I follow where You lead
me. In Jesus' Name, Amen.

Day 15: **The Opposition To God's Plan**

"And so we sent Timothy, our brother and God's servant in [spreading] the good news of Christ, to strengthen and encourage you [exhorting, comforting, and establishing you] in regard to your faith, so that no one would be unsettled by these difficulties [to which I have referred]. For you know that we have been destined for this [as something unavoidable in our position]." - 1Thessalonians 3:2-3 (AMP)

A question was posed about the difficulties we sometimes face as we walk out God's plan for our life. First, we must be mindful of the words of Jesus in John 16:33. He said, "In the world, you shall have tribulation."

Not maybe, or a possibility, but He said that we would be met with all types of difficulties meant to stop a born-again believer from walking in the fullness of what God has called the individual to do. After we have sought the counsel of God for direction and guidance for our life and begun to walk out the plan God has for us, we can be assured, according to the words of Jesus, that we will be met with opposition.

Understand you can be right in the middle of God's will and find yourself in all kinds of trouble. Jesus was walking in the will of God as the bible states in Matthew 20:28 that He came to give His life as a ransom and found Himself in all kinds of trouble.

"just as the Son of Man did not come to be served, but to serve, and to give His life as a ransom for many [paying the price to set them free from the penalty of sin].” – Matthew 20:28 (AMP)

With all that Paul had to face, he was in the will of God according to Acts 9:15,16 (NKJV), which says, “…for he is a chosen vessel unto me, to bear my name before the Gentiles, and kings, and the children of Israel; For I will show him how great things he must suffer for my name's sake.”

Because of the right motive and our heart being set on doing the will of God, we walk out the plan of God in the face of opposition, knowing that we are seeking to fulfill what God has chosen for our life. We will find ourselves filled with peace when it is God's plan for us, regardless of what we may be facing. Be careful to see that before Jesus told the disciples about the tribulation they must face, He said that we could have perfect peace in Him.

Peace is the distinguishing factor of whether or not we are walking according to God's plan or one we have devised on our own and are looking for Him to co-sign it. The plan that He has devised for your life is the one that will bring peace and stability into your life even when you face opposition. Whenever you are outside God's will for your life, you will meet with struggle simply created because you are trying to operate in your own strength; therefore, you will have no peace.

There will be no struggle when it is God's plan and in His season, but there will be opposition, and our text says that it is our appointed lot to have difficulties and opposition when walking according to the plan of God. So, understand that even when walking in the plan of God for your life, you will have opposition, but know that you will have peace within that keeps you grounded and settled as you continue to walk in what God has called you to do for the Kingdom.

Father, thank You for equipping me
within with Your peace to look into the
face of opposition and continue to walk
in what You have planned for my life.
Thank You for the strength and courage
You have given me to do Your will. In
Jesus' Name, Amen.

Day 16: **Take That Next Step**

"Wherefore seeing we also are compassed about with so great a cloud of witnesses, let us lay aside every weight, and the sin which doth so easily beset us, and let us run with patience the race that is set before us," - Hebrews 12:1 (KJV)

For every born-again believer on a journey in life, there is always that one thing we must do to propel us into the place God has destined for us to be. We are all born with a purpose in life and must set our will and determination to reach that place. When we look at this passage of scripture, it begins by concluding from the previous chapter that we have been surrounded by a great cloud of witnesses of faith but precedes to tell us that we must, to fulfill our calling in life, move beyond that one thing which so easily besets us; which means that thing which prevents us and our plans (God ordained plan) from being successful.

This race, which we mention, is the assignment God has given to each of us to operate in life so that we do our part in promoting the Kingdom of God and sharing this gospel of grace here on earth. That weight and sin are those things in our life that always seems to loom to keep us from taking that next step. We want to enter that secret place with God where we are effective in fulfilling our calling.

It may be fear, feelings of inadequacy, or a lack of trust that prevents us from taking that next step we feel within us, but we must be willing to lay it aside and become that living sacrifice which is our reasonable service and have the mindset which gets us into our place of calling. When we received our salvation, God began a work within us, symbolic of the Tabernacle. We began in the outer court and, through prayer and study of His Word, moved into the inner court with Him, but ultimately need to get into the Holy of Holies.

Every level brings about more resistance when you walk by faith, so it is a sin and weight that hinders us from taking that next step toward God. It is not the lack of faith that hinders us, but that one thing, whatever it is, which causes us to squander the opportunities presented. The weight and sin inhibit us from making that all-important decision to move, which is what we must overcome to take that next step with God.

First, we must identify our weight and sin, which easily beset us, then follow the instructions in Hebrews 12:2, which say we are to be "looking away from all that will distract to Jesus…."

Keeping our eyes fixed and focused on Jesus allows us to move forward with the confidence and assurance that we can do all things through Christ. In Matthew 14, Peter took a step of faith with his eyes on Jesus, but Matthew 14:30 says, "But when he saw the winds boisterous, he was afraid…."

Whatever that one thing is that has you stagnant, lay it aside, fix your focus on Jesus, and Take The Next Step.

Father, thank You today for the
resolve and confidence You are building
in me to move into that place You have
prepared just for me. Help me to identify
that one thing in my life that has so easily

*beset me so that I set it aside and run this
race and reach the destination that has
been preordained for me. In Jesus' Name,
Amen.*

Day 17: **Equipped For Battle**

"For Thou has girded me with strength unto the battle: Thou has subdued under me those who rose up against me." - Psalm 18:39 (KJV)

Thinking back to when I first read Psalm 18 and understood that David wrote this when it said that the Lord had delivered him from all his enemies, I thought of the day when God would deliver me from all my enemies. Then, I read John 16:33, where Jesus told the disciples they should have tribulation in this world. Not maybe, or there is a good chance, but if you choose this way of life which I am going to die for you to obtain, then be prepared because you will be met with opposition, test and trials which will try to move you from this abundant life My death will provide for you if you choose to follow Me.

Today I can truly say that in my heart, I understand there is a rest for me in this life of faith, but it does not exempt me from the subtle and constant attacks from the enemy. Just as I have a purpose and destiny to which I am striving to reach, Satan also has the assignment to try and prevent me from getting to that set or appointed place. But the good news is that although the battle may be fierce and riddled with pain, our text says that we who have placed our trust in Jesus have been equipped for the battles we must face.

On the run, being hunted like a criminal and away from everything dear to him (1 Samuel), David held on to his integrity and continued to trust God because although the going got tough for him and his men, he knew that he had an appointment with destiny that he was ordained to keep.

So, knowing that he would make it to his expected end, he came to understand and penned the words, "Thou has girded me with strength unto the battle." He understood that it was God who was keeping and protecting him as he was walking through this valley which had the resemblance of death (Psalm 23:4).

There were opportunities presented which could have allowed David to avenge himself, but he chose to trust God to subdue his enemies under him, and of course, God did. Oh, the test we must face as we walk out this life of faith, but we must always remember that God has equipped us for the battles we must face so that He receives the glory due Him from our lives of obedience to and trust in Him.

Understand that the attacks come with the assignment that God has given you, but He is so awesome that He placed within you the resolve to withstand them and press your way to your place of destiny. Don't fret or complain about the things coming against you; just remember that God has girded, which means to prepare you for conflict or vigorous activity, endowed you with the strength to withstand these attacks and bring Him the glory as you stand by faith with wholehearted trust in Him.

*Father, thank You for equipping me
with the grace I need to walk through my
fiery furnace and continue on the path
You have set me on so that I finish my
course with joy and bring glory and
honor to Your name, Amen.*

Day 18: **Preparation For Ministry**

"And I thank Christ Jesus our Lord, who hath enabled me, for that He counted me faithful, putting me into the ministry." - 1 Timothy 1:12 (KJV)

While listening to an awesome sermon on loyalty and commitment, I held to the statement that God calls us to Himself before He sends us out to do ministry work. I thought that the first step into ministry is giving your heart to God and listening to Him. Proverbs 23:26 explains this call when He says, "My son, give Me thine heart, and let thine eyes observe My ways." The loyalty and commitment needed to serve God come from a heart submitted to Him out of love.

Remember, all believers are called, but not all are chosen. So, understand that when God calls, He will test you to see if you are worthy to be chosen. A call will not qualify you, but you must be faithful to the call before you are chosen. This may seem contradictory to the omniscience of God, but He must try his heart to see if you have given it to Him. We can never be faithful and loyal to the call unless we have first given Him our hearts. Therefore, God will take you through a series of tests to prepare you for this ministry work.

The first one is the Time Test. When God calls you, He will first put you on the shelf and leave you there. He has already spoken to you and made the call, so now He will shut every door in your face to turn your dependence to Him because Proverbs 19:21 says, "Many plans are in a man's mind, but it is the Lord's purpose for him that will stand."

He will ignore you to check your motives and then purify them. He searches your heart by putting you on the shelf and leaving you there for a season to see how you handle the waiting. If you stick with the call, your faith will grow. He has placed you there to build your faith to where your total dependency is on Him.

What you are going through is a season of waiting, which is necessary for development. God wants your heart submitted to Him in love so that your eyes only observe and follow His ways. Keep in mind that time gives birth to faith. This is the first step of your preparation, so do not grow weary in the time test; rather, keep your focus on God and trust Him as your development begins right here in this test.

Father, thank you for Your sufficient
and sustaining grace which keeps me
during my season of waiting. Fill me with
the knowledge of Your will for my life in
all wisdom and spiritual understanding.
In Jesus' Name, Amen.

Day 19: **Make The Word Your Source**

"My son, attend to my words; incline thine ear unto my sayings. Let them not depart from thine eyes; keep them in the midst of thine heart." - Proverbs 4:20-21 (KJV)

Yesterday we started looking at the various tests God will take you through to prepare you for ministry. We infringed on the thought that God always calls you to Himself before He sends you out and will test you to see if you are worthy of the call. In this preparation, we saw that the loyalty and commitment needed to serve Him faithfully comes from a heart submitted to Him out of love. Remember that everyone is called, but not all are chosen.

Understanding your calling from God isn't a one-and-done deal; it's a journey filled with trials and revelations. It's like a refining fire, purifying you, ensuring you are truly devoted and fit for His purpose. While this may seem contradictory given God's omniscience, remember that He examines the heart to ensure its complete surrender to Him, not to know its depth.

Complete loyalty and faithfulness to His call can only emerge from a heart fully given to Him. Thus, God, in His wisdom, orchestrates a series of tests uniquely designed to prepare you for the divine assignment He has for you.

One critical test you will encounter on this journey is the Word Test. This test probes the depth of your scriptural knowledge and, more importantly, your reliance on it. Life will throw situations your way, offering you a choice— lean on the Word of God, treating it as the ultimate authority, or rely on your intellect to reason them out.

So, when faced with these challenges, where will you turn? Will God's Word be your compass, guiding your actions? This is the question that the Word Test seeks to answer. Remember, these tests aren't designed to dishearten you; they are meant to strengthen your bond with God and reaffirm your commitment to His divine purpose.

God wants to know that you will turn to the Word for your answers to what you are confronted with. This will be when you can rely on nothing but the Word of God. When Joseph went through his season of adversity (Genesis 39), he held to the Word of God and walked through his troubles with the godly integrity he had within. Psalm 105:17-19 says, "He sent a man before them, even Joseph, who was sold for a servant: Whose feet they hurt with fetters: he was laid in iron: Until the time that His Word came: the Word of the Lord tried him."

The Word of God must become your only source. The Psalmist gives clear instructions on navigating through this life of faith; by giving our attention to the Word. The Word of God must be the guide you use if you are to be successful. Psalm 119:105 says, Your Word is a lamp to my feet and a light to my path." The Word of God gives understanding and clarity for the journey. We are instructed to meditate on it day and night; therefore, to be effective in ministry, let there be no doubt that you must be a student of the Word.

Father, today I thank You for sending
Your Word to heal and deliver me from

*my destruction. Help me make Your Word
the final authority for everything I face in
this life. In Jesus' Name, Amen.*

Day 20: **Under Fire**

"Beloved, think it not strange concerning the fiery trial which is to try you, as though some strange thing happened unto you:" - 1 Peter 4:12 (KJV)

Today, we will take a side journey and add a new but profound truth to our topic of Preparation for Ministry. As we have already discussed some of the various tests God will walk you through to equip you for your calling, it seems important to warn you that this anointing on your life will attract attacks.

Yes, the enemy has set out to stop you from fulfilling your calling, but you must see it differently. There is a war test that God will take you through in which you will have to fight, and we will come to it later, but right now, grab hold of the thought that with this anointing, God's favor and enablement which is upon you, it will attract attacks, and the most prevalent will come from the people around you.

Unbeknownst to them, Satan has used his subtle tactics of deception and deceit. He will find a way to sow discord and what a Pastor friend calls spiritual jealousy into their thinking. I say thinking because he will use self-deception, the most dangerous form of deception, to cause them to see their error and disobedience in you.

Understand that God's divine anointing bestowed upon you is akin to a beacon, perceptible to those around you. This visible blessing will elicit a spectrum of reactions. On one end, it will attract individuals who genuinely appreciate and celebrate your gifts, their hearts filled with gratitude and joy.

Conversely, on the other end, it can also draw in detractors who may envy your divine endowment. Some among these may even harbor the belief that they are more deserving of these spiritual gifts. Thus, the anointing path is graced by admiration and marked by challenges.

But God is no respecter of person, and Romans 11:29 Amplified says that "God's gifts and His call are irrevocable. He never withdraws them once they are given, and He does not change His mind about those to whom He gives His grace or sends His call."

God calls us to Himself and then chooses who and how He desires to use us to fulfill His purpose on earth. And although He is just, His favor is not fair. That said, know that you will only draw those attacks that God has already determined you can handle. So, He tells us in Ezekiel 3:8-9: "Behold I have made thy face (presence) strong against their faces (presence), and thy forehead (conspicuousness) strong against their foreheads. As an adamant harder than flint have I made thy forehead: fear them not, neither be dismayed at their looks…"

The word conspicuous means easily or clearly visible, attracting attention through being unusual or remarkable. It carries the idea of being open and prominent, meaning you will be sticking out, noticeable, and well-known. It's not that you are trying to be seen. It's just that the anointing on you will be glowing, thus making it noticeable to others and attracting attacks. Although you may be under fire because of your anointing, you must focus on Jesus and the cross, which reminds you of your VICTORY.

Father, thank You for the grace You have given me to walk in Your anointing and the strength You provide so that I stand in the face of every opposition, knowing that I always triumph in Your Son, Christ Jesus. Amen.

Day 21: **The Wilderness Test**

"And thou shalt remember all the way which the Lord thy God led thee these forty years in the wilderness, to humble thee, and to prove thee, to know what was in thine heart, whether thou wouldest Keep His commandments or no." - Deuteronomy 8:2 (KJV)

The eighth chapter of Deuteronomy holds a special place in my spiritual journey. I refer to it as my "Guard Against Pride" chapter, an ever-present reminder to remain humble amidst the blessings bestowed upon me by God.

This chapter resonates deeply because it echoes a pivotal moment in my life. I sought divine intervention during a challenging situation, and God always provided. Yet, instead of attributing the resolution to His grace, I let pride seep in and convinced myself that I was the architect of my success.

In essence, Deuteronomy's eighth chapter serves as my constant beacon of humility, cautioning me not to let the blessings I receive create a veil of pride and self-acclaim. It reminds me that my achievements are not solely my own but the fruit of divine grace. This realization keeps my pride in check, ensuring I never forget the true source of my blessings.

What I didn't realize then is that the world still held me and called me right back to the things my flesh desired, with the goods that God, in my time of distress and at my request, had blessed me with. I lived in this condition for about eight years before this world of false security fell apart, and once again, I had to cry out to God for help.

As we read in the Old Testament, the story of God delivering the children of Israel out of Egypt, they indeed left Egypt, but Egypt was still in them, preventing them from accepting the provisions God provided for them. They kept holding on to what they had in Egypt and could not see God's desire to bless them. For the believer, Egypt represents the world, and as long as the world, which is full of cares and deceitfulness of riches, and lusts, has a hold on you, it will choke the Word of God out of you (Mark 4:19) and take you down a path of pending destruction.

So to prepare for what He has called me to do required me to go through a series of tests, and the one we will discuss today is called the wilderness test. This wilderness test I found to be the most difficult of them all. Before God could use Moses to lead these people out of Egypt, he had to spend forty years on a mountain tending sheep to strip Egypt out of him. When Moses answered God's call, he lost his desire for the things that Egypt provided him growing up in the palace of Pharaoh.

That time alone out in the wilderness caused him to be stripped of that world system. It did not matter to him anymore, for he needed to understand the call on his life. The wilderness test is when you lose everything and find yourself alone with God. You lose your dependence on others and the false security you once lived with. You need answers for your life, and you will only find them in God and His Word. You will find yourself in a dry place which will motivate you to seek the Lord in a consistent and committed life of prayer and His Word. In your wilderness is where you learn to trust God to sustain your life.

Trust in God's process: it's designed to guide you toward spiritual clarity and emotional resilience. As challenging as it may seem, this journey prepares you to rely wholeheartedly on Him, cleansing your mind and hcart from worldly distractions. It helps you tune into the divine whispers intended solely for you.

Yes, this phase can be daunting, but remember what God reveals in Deuteronomy 8:16: this trying time is a test, a prerequisite to the bountiful goodness that awaits you in your later years. It's a humbling journey, molding you to befit the Master's purpose, as highlighted below:

"Therefore, if anyone cleanses himself from the latter, he will be a vessel for honor, sanctified and useful for the Master, prepared for every good work." - 2 Timothy 2:21 (NKJV)

Don't scorn this transformative process, as the Children of Israel did in the wilderness. Instead, embrace the journey and anticipate the rewards that lie ahead. It's not just about surviving the wilderness but flourishing on the other side of it.

Father, thank You for the process I
must go through to prepare me to best
serve You and the kingdom. I know You
will walk me through this and comfort me
with Your love when it seems I can't make
it. Help me maintain a good attitude and

too always focus on Your promises.
Amen.

Day 22: **The Servant Test**

"And if you have not been faithful in that which is another man's, who shall give you that which is your own."
- Luke 16:12 (NKJV)

A few days ago, we started looking at the various tests God will take you through to prepare you for ministry. We infringed on the thought that God always calls you to Himself before He sends you out and will test you to see if you are worthy of the call. In this preparation, we saw that the loyalty and commitment needed to serve Him faithfully comes from a heart submitted to Him out of love. Remember that everyone is called, but not all are chosen.

Understand this clearly; when God calls, He will test you to see if you are worthy to be chosen. Although this may seem contradictory to the omniscience of God, bear in mind that He must try your heart to see if you have given it to Him. We can never be faithful and loyal to the call unless we have given Him our heart; therefore, God will take you through a series of tests to prepare you for this ministry work.

The next test we will briefly examine is the Servant Test. God will put you in place to see if you will serve another Pastor or ministry. God wants to see if you will be faithful to another chosen vessel before He will trust you with your own. Can you faithfully serve another with the same faithfulness required for your own? Can this man trust you to follow and do what he needs you to do? Know this; The man of God you are serving may be unpredictable.

He could pull away from you when he is going through his issues, and God is testing you to see if you will serve the man even when he is extremely difficult. God is testing your limit to stay strong and continue to serve this man of God even when it becomes uncomfortable, and you disagree with Him.

He wants to see if you will trust God in the man. God wants to see if your motivation for ministry is just to be seen in the public eye or if you are dependable and accountable to accept and complete the most menial task with a spirit of excellence. The test is to see if you can remain faithful to the call even when it does not appear to fit your expectation of what your role should be at present.

Can you sit when it appears you should be doing more? Have you accepted this as a time of preparation and that serving beneath what you feel God has called you to is a test of your commitment to service? God wants to see if you will be faithful in the little before He trusts you with greater.

Father, thank You for the faithfulness
that You have shown me and for all that
You are doing within me to be the servant
that You have called me to be. Amen.

Day 23: **The Patience Test**

"To everything, there is a season, A time for every purpose under heaven:" - Ecclesiastes 3:1 (NKJV)

As we explore various tests that God leads us through in preparation for ministry work, a thought emerges with profound clarity: God's call always beckons us to Himself before He propels us outwards. Therefore, it becomes crucial to recognize that God's tests are not arbitrary but measure the worthiness of this call.

An understanding unfolds in this preparation phase. The loyalty and commitment required to serve Him faithfully are not imposed obligations but emanate from a heart that submits to Him out of love. This submission becomes a distinguishing factor: while everyone may be called, not all are chosen.

Indeed, it may seem paradoxical in the face of God's omniscience: why would an all-knowing entity need to test us? But it is essential to remember that God scrutinizes the heart, exploring whether we have truly surrendered to Him. The significance of surrender cannot be understated. We can't exhibit fidelity and loyalty to the call without handing over our hearts. Hence, God guides us through tests to prepare us for this consequential ministry work. In this process, we establish our readiness and worthiness for the divine call.

We last looked at the Servant Test. We discussed how God would put you in place to see if you would serve another Pastor or ministry. God wants to see if you will be faithful to another chosen vessel before He will trust you with your own. Can you faithfully serve another with the same faithfulness required for your own? Can this man trust you to follow and do what he needs you to do? We concluded that He is testing your limit to stay strong and continue to serve this man of God even when it becomes uncomfortable and you disagree with Him. He wants to see if you will trust God in the man.

Next is the Patience Test. God wants to see that while you are serving another, you can be patient and not begin to question when your time has come. You must prove to God that you are a patient man and trust Him to equip and prepare you for your chosen assignment. You must have the patience to allow God to equip you with the spiritual understanding you need to minister to people.

Patience allows God to perfect things that pertain to you and the character development needed to function in this capacity. While He is working His good pleasure within you so that you can be effective in the place He has chosen to send you, He needs to see you display a level of trust in Him that allows you to rest in your current position and wait for Him to move you.

Never can we get ahead of God's timing because of our impatience. I have found patience to be a key attribute for God's chosen vessels. We never want to get ahead of God; rather, we must patiently watch and wait as He opens the door of opportunity for us. Promotion comes only from God and requires His servant to operate by allowing patience to have its perfect work in this process.

Never decide that you are ready to walk into what God has spoken to you, but be patient and allow Him to move you when He determines everything is in place so that His purpose is fulfilled.

Father, I want to thank you today for instilling the patience to wait for Your perfect timing so that I fulfill Your will for my life. Open the eyes of my understanding today so that I truly and correctly discern when You are ready for me to move. In Jesus' Name, Amen.

Day 24: **Free of Frustration**

"Therefore, we do not become discouraged [spiritless, disappointed, or afraid]. Though our outer self is [progressively] wasting away, yet our inner self is being [progressively] renewed day by day." - 2 Corinthians 4:16 (AMP)

To continue with the series of tests that God will take you through to prepare you for works of ministry, the Frustration Test can prove to be painful. These tests are not singled out and given separately but occur simultaneously. As you are amid the Word Test' and digging into the Word for answers, the loneliness of the Wilderness Test will begin to mount, and you will find yourself becoming more uncomfortable and forced into another level of prayer because of the mounting questions in your thinking. At this point, you must seek an intimacy with God that begins to move you beyond what you were accustomed to.

In the Servant Test, you may find that the load is seemingly unbearable as you serve another Pastor while holding to the vision God has placed in you, and in and through it all, you must be patient to prove to God that you are trusting Him and His timing. This gets us to our next test, which is the Frustration Test. With all that you are going through in this process of change and development, you will become so frustrated with your life that your body will ache from the pressure, and your mind will get tired because Hebrews 12:3 says you must endure to avoid being wearied and fainting in your mind.

Anytime you live beneath your purpose, you will become frustrated, but you have to understand that God is trying your heart and mind to see if you are worthy of your calling. These tests are not to destroy you but to build the resolve you need to stand up against the weight of your calling. The frustration comes because your soul is being pressured by your flesh, seeing it wants to take control and be free of the turmoil you are experiencing during this period of transformation. The frustration comes with the uncertainties that are a part of God stretching you beyond your comfort to prepare you for the work He has called you to. The potential for stress is there if you do not focus on your destiny and constantly remind yourself that patience is a key attribute in this preparation process.

Don't lose focus of where you are going, but endure your days of nothingness; when you have expended energy and effort, and nothing seems to be happening. Keep your eyes on the end, and walk through this period in your life Free of Frustration.

Father, I thank You for comforting
my heart when I find myself in a troubled
place. Fill me with the knowledge of Your
will and lead me according to the path
You have chosen to walk without any
frustration. Amen.

Day 25: **The Discouragement Test**

"Behold, the Lord thy God hath set the land before thee: go up and possess it, as the Lord God of thy fathers hath said unto thee; fear not, neither be discouraged." - Deuteronomy 1:21 (KJV)

As you have entered that place of frustration, you will become discouraged because of the nothingness you see from your expended energy and effort as you press your way into what you know God has called you to do. Anytime you live beneath your purpose, there is the potential for frustration if you lose focus and become impatient with the process, which takes you into promise.

If you allow it, the frustration will cause you to become discouraged, losing your confidence and motivation because of where you are. As we mentioned earlier, these tests all work simultaneously to build within you the tenacity to press your way through every hindrance and stand up against the weights of life. The discouragement you begin to experience will make you feel like you want to quit and die. You will become tired of the time, the work, the energy, and the effort you put in during this transformation process.

What God is doing in this test is helping you to refocus on the call. The frustration comes, and this eventually will cause you to reexamine your priorities. Remember that these tests are not to destroy you but are intended to build in you the resolve that you need to stand up against the weight of what your calling requires.

Remenber, the frustration comes because your soul, which is being pressured by your flesh, wants to take control and be free of the turmoil you are experiencing during this period of transformation. The frustration leads you to this discouragement because of the uncertainties that are part of the process of God stretching you beyond your comfort to ensure you are adequately prepared for the work He has called you to.

Lastly, understand that disappointments are inevitable on this journey, but discouragement is your choice. Therefore, we want to encourage you to recognize the tests you find yourself in, keep your face set like flint to the place of your calling, and endure hardness as the good soldier you have been called to be.

Father, I want to thank You for the strength that You give to the faint in heart to stay the course and continue to trust in Your power and might. Thank You for the indwelling Spirit Who bears witness to my spirit and encourages me to press my way into my destiny. In Jesus' Name, Amen.

Day 26: **The War Test**

"He teaches my hands to make war, So that my arms can bend a bow of bronze." - Psalm 18:34 (NKJV)

Whenever I read Psalm 18, it always motivates me because David penned this after he had endured the persecution and trial that drove Him into the wilderness for years to escape King Saul, who wanted him dead. After all, he knew that God had chosen David to be king in his stead. David was known as a fighter throughout his life, from when he tended his father's sheep, engaged in and defeated Goliath, and throughout the numerous battles, he fought as he ran for his life. In our text, David says that God taught his hands to war.

Remember that David was anointed to be king over Israel at the young age of seventeen, but the preparation required to step into his destiny took place over thirteen years, in which he had to fight. Imagine the frustration he must have felt and the discouragement from seeing everything contrary to what he was promised happening in his life. On top of that, he had opportunities to kill his enemy (King Saul) and step into his promised kingship, yet he endured the Patience Test and chose to wait on God's timing to bring him into his appointed place.

This now is the War Test, where God will test your fighting abilities. Here you learn if you are willing to fight the good fight of faith daily. God wants to develop your spiritual weapons and warfare abilities because regardless of how intense the battle is to get you into your place of promise, He knows you will face greater battles once you reach that place.

The only way out is to engage in this spiritual battle and fight. He has provided us with the tools to fight, but we must possess the resolve to engage in the battle, appropriate what He has made available to us, and endure to the end. He needs to know that we will fight for what He has promised.

One of my favorite scriptures is Jude 2b, where the writer says we must contend for the faith. The word "contend" implies that we must struggle with an adversary. Some synonyms are fight, labor fervently, and strive. We must do this in the War Test; fight for everything God has promised us, even when facing frustration and discouragement. Now is the time to dig in your heels and truly fight the good fight of faith.

Father, I want to thank You for equipping me with what I need to fight a battle that has already been won. Give me the grace to take a stand and contend for the faith given unto me. Today I go in your strength and engage in this battle before my promise. Amen.

Day 27: **Light The Way**

"But the path of the just is as the shining light, that shineth more and more unto the perfect day." - Proverbs 4:18 (KJV)

At a point in my life, while contemplating the changes happening to me, I ran across a quote by Dr. Charles Stanley which gave me some understanding, or should I say clarity, about the path I am now traveling. He said that "God does not require us to understand His will, just obey it, even if it seems unreasonable."

How many of us think that because we don't understand what is evolving in our life, we have an excuse to be cautious and become stagnant when God calls us to move in a direction that leads into another dimension of His plan for our life?

What our text reveals for those of us who will take that step of faith and move even when we don't understand is that the path becomes brighter as we move forward in faith. He says that the path of the just, the one God has declared to be in right standing with Him, and called according to His purpose, is a shining light, meaning your path will become clearer with each step of faith you take.

The direction God is taking you may seem unreasonable, impossible to achieve, and beyond your capabilities, but He has promised if we just walk in faith, the light will become brighter and brighter as we walk. With time we will get a clearer understanding of what He is doing in your life. As God lights the way you build the confidence and courage to take the next step with ease many times with no visible evidence that you are in line with His will. But as Dr. Stanley said, He does not require us to understand it but rather to obey it regardless of what our finite thinking tries to convey to us.

Faith is stepping out on nothing and believing God for everything. As we walk by faith, the eyes of our understanding will be enlightened as we go. Psalm 32:8 (KJV) says of God, "I will instruct thee and teach thee in the way which thou shalt go: I will guide thee with mine eye."

God will ensure that your pathway is illuminated with each step so that you begin to see your journey from His perspective, which is all according to His will so that His purpose is fulfilled. God does not intend for you to regress because you don't understand His plan for you, so with each step, He sheds more light on what He intends and desires so that you begin to see your way clearer.

Another quote Dr. Stanley used is this: "Obey God and leave all the consequences to Him." Just like car insurance, for any accident, you may have while on this journey, God has you fully insured and is responsible for you when you walk by faith. Keep walking even when you don't understand, and God will Light The Way.

Father, thank You for leading and
guiding me along the path You have
chosen for me to walk and making my
way clearer with each step of faith. In
Jesus' Name, I Pray, Amen.

Day 28: **Will You Stand Alone?**

"But the Lord stood by me and strengthened and empowered me, so that through me the [gospel] message might be fully proclaimed, and that all the Gentiles might hear it; and I was rescued from the mouth of the lion." - 2 Timothy 4:17 (NKJV)

Have you ever dreamed a dream that seemed so ridiculous that you couldn't tell anyone, or they just gave you that little "hum" when you did? Maybe the dream was so big that it seemed to be unreasonable. These are the kinds of dreams that others just won't accept. They can't imagine God doing something this great for you because they can't get past what they think about you or your past. This becomes the kind of dream that many will back away from simply because it will not give you the support you need to fulfill it. But this kind of dream is not dependent on what others may think about it; rather, it depends on you believing and trusting God to bring it to pass.

The feeling of wanting others to share this dream with you will soon become a fading thought as you prayerfully seek understanding about this dream and its purpose. Everyone around you has not only rejected your dream because they can't seem to fathom the thought of you doing it but all of your help will be prevented from helping you. God wants to receive all the glory for you doing something you on your own can't do.

So, when others reject your dream, you have no help, and there is absolutely nothing you can do to bring this dream to pass; God only wants to know if you will stand alone. God has given you something unobtainable on your own, but your willingness to believe Him, even if you have to stand alone, will guide you to fulfill this dream and do all He has placed in your heart to do.

In the book of Genesis, chapter 37, God gave Joseph a dream that caused his brothers to hate him for it and also be rebuked by his father. Yet he held on to his dream through years of adversity, never becoming offended by God, and continued to honor and serve Him because he had decided to stand alone with this dream. Everything that happens as you await God to bring this dream to pass is merely a tool the enemy will use to get you to abandon your dream.

Dreams that are too big to dream are dreams only God can give. They are not meant to be understood and accepted by others, but because you know that God gave you this dream, it is the fuel that drives you to press forward, trusting God to bring it to pass. As the dream begins to unfold with each progressive step, you understand more and more and soon realize that if God does not help you, you are guaranteed to fail. But since it was given to you by Him, and you have stood on the dream, God will do all He has promised He would do to bring it to pass.

Don't worry about what others say about your dream; continue to trust God and stand, even if you have to stand alone. A word of wisdom, sometimes you may need to silently pursue your dreams without sharing them with others. But even if you have to stand alone, don't stop dreaming.

Father, thank You for all You have placed in my heart to do for Your kingdom. As I pursue this dream, lead, and guide me according to what You have purposed for me to do without reservation or concern, knowing that You will make every provision. Today, I thank You for all that You will do to bring this dream to pass. In Jesus' Name, Amen.

Day 29: **When God Speaks**

" And they said unto Moses, Speak thou with us, and we will hear: but let not God speak with us, lest we die." - Exodus 20:19 (KJV)

I can remember sharing on one occasion about having a season of adversity in which it seems as if everything is coming against you, and there just seems to be no end to the trouble in your life. The trials come one after another with such destructive force that all you can do is cry out to God to give you the grace to persevere through it. The one thing we should seek during this time is a Word from God. We spend time with God and His Word daily so that we are prepared to face these times of trouble with the Word of God hidden in our hearts to strengthen us and give us the courage and comfort to press through because of what it says about the trouble that we will face on this journey.

But we should seek a Word from God during this season, which will cause a breakthrough. When everything is coming against you, and you are standing on the Word of God, fighting the good fight of faith, and God speaks a Word to you right in the midst of that trial, you will experience an overwhelming sense of victory because of the assuring words your Father just spoke to you. The weight of that trial will be lifted at that very moment because when God speaks to His children, your confidence rises to another level, and your faith is strengthened, causing a breakthrough right in the middle of that thing.

Right then, that trouble means nothing because when God speaks to you, it is to confirm that He is faithful and will perform everything He said in His Word concerning your trouble. When God speaks to you and confirms that Word you have hidden in your heart and was standing on, it takes on new life, and you are strengthened to rise and stare that trouble right in the face and speak words of faith to it. A man that has heard from God cannot be defeated. He will not be moved off the Word of God because he has just received a Word from God and is energized with more confidence to run on, assured of victory. A Word from God is a breakthrough because everything that He said in His Word about trouble in the life of a believer has just been confirmed, and the victory validated.

After having seasons of adversities in my own life and seeking a Word from God in the midst of it, then hearing those comforting words from Him, I thought about the children of Israel in this chapter and what caused them to not want to hear God's voice. I won't elaborate on this thought, but I can only say that it is refreshing and comforting to hear from God. When God speaks, it warms your heart, and you will experience His love in a new way. His words are a stamp of approval and remove any shadow of doubt that tries to convince you that God is not with you.

Every time that I have found myself in what I call a world of trouble, God always sheds light on the situation when He spoke His words of approval and turned the entire situation around. Seeking to hear God's voice is a practice that Christians must continue to cultivate in our lives. When everything looks dark, and you can't see a way out, a breakthrough usually follows: When God Speaks.

Father, teach me to hear Your voice in my times of trouble. Let Your spoken words cause breakthroughs in my situations, and may I always have a song of praise in my mouth for all the wonderful things that You do. In Jesus' Name, Amen.

Day 30: **Your Own Portion**

"…..every man gathered according to his need." - Exodus 16:18 (AMP)

When I looked around, I found that many start on this Christian journey, but it seems few will walk faithfully and with/in obedience. This puzzles me at times about the needs of an individual. Although we all know what it is we need to be successful and walk uprightly before the Lord, we must at the same time be careful to understand that not everyone will have the same desire that you do, even though your heart goes out with passion to see all come into the knowledge of the truth.

Only you know what God delivered you from and how far He had to bring you. I once said that when God's anointing is on you, it will take you to higher levels of maturity and at each level, the air gets thinner and not all can breathe at that altitude, so you must leave some behind.

Mark 4:24 (AMP) reads, "Then He said to them, "Pay attention to what you hear. By your own standard of measurement [that is, to the extent that you study spiritual truth and apply godly wisdom], it will be measured to you [and you will be given even greater ability to respond]—and more will be given to you besides."

Not everyone desires to move to greater levels of maturity in the things of God as you do. Your prayer life may be one that others think is excessive and not required, but you must continue to seek the portion of knowledge and virtue that you need to be pleasing to God in all that you do for Him. If you only want to be a stay-in-the-boat Christian and just make it to heaven, you will only seek what is necessary to maintain that simple desire.

On the other hand, if you have a passion to be used by God to promote the kingdom of God, then He has a larger portion available for you. In our text, he told Moses to instruct the people to gather according to their needs. Some of us have a greater need than others and will put forth the effort to receive it.

Some of us receive our new birth at an early age, and even though we all will have struggles in life, there are those like myself who have lived out in the world for many years and has a greater need of God's goodness in my life to stay in this way that He has called me to. My portion also may be greater according to the call that I have accepted. Those that get out of the boat will require a greater portion than those who sit safely in it.

Ask yourself today, what portion do I require? Have I decided to stay safely in the boat and only gather a little understanding, or do I need a larger portion because my desire for the things of God requires me to obtain a larger portion?

Of the twelve Apostles, we only hear of a few who greatly impacted the New Testament church. Peter, James, and John needed a larger portion of God's grace to fulfill the work that was given to them. Not that the others did not, but these had a greater need and gathered according to that need. We must evaluate what we desire and then go after the portion we need to fulfill it.

God has made His grace available to us all, but He knows that not all will desire to serve Him in a greater capacity, so He tells us to get Your Own Portion.

Father, thank You for making Your goodness available to me to gather according to my need to fulfill the desire to serve You. Take me from one level of maturity to the next so that I may serve You in a greater capacity. Help me to understand that not everyone will have the need that I do, and give me the heart to help draw them to what You are calling me to. In Jesus' Name, I Pray, Amen.

Conclusion: Whose Plan Is It?

"For I know the plans and thoughts that I have for you,' says the Lord, 'plans for peace and well-being and not for disaster, to give you a future and a hope." - Jeremiah 29:11 (AMP)

Today I was reminded of a statement that I made to someone about the decisions we tend to make in life according to our finite knowledge and understanding. We take what we call a good idea and devise these plans for our life without consulting God, and then proceed to seek to have it endorsed by Him later.

We end up with a good idea, but not a 'God idea,' and usually totally out of His plan for our life. Then we find ourselves out there operating in our own strength, trying to work out a plan that was our own, asking God to finance and direct it when He had no desire for you to be in it in the first place. God already has a plan for our life, and we should seek Him to discover what it is. Otherwise, we will go from one idea to the next without lasting results.

God told Jeremiah in 1:5 (KJV), "Before I formed thee in the belly I knew thee; and before thou camest forth out of the womb I sanctified thee, and I ordained thee a prophet unto the nations."

God had a plan for his life before he was ever born. Imagine him trying to do anything other than what was ordained for his life; he would have experienced one dead end after another. This is the importance of spending time with God: He will direct your path to that which He purposed for your life. Second Timothy 1:9 (NKJV) confirms that He "called us with a holy calling, not according to our works, but according to His own purpose and grace."

The plan that He has devised for your life is the one that will bring peace and stability into your life. Anytime you are outside of the will of God for your life, you will meet with an opposing force simply created because you are trying to operate in your strength, and the bible says that without God, you can do nothing (John 15:5), but that you can do all things through and by Christ Jesus (Philippians 4:13).

There will be no struggle when it is God's plan and in His season. Everything for our life has already been prepared, and we must now discover what He has chosen for us to do. Hebrews 12:1 says to "run with patience the race that is set before us", and all we must do is acknowledge Him in all our ways, and He promises to direct our path (Proverbs 3:6).

Our one and only desire should be to do what God wants us to do in this life. So many years of our lives have been wasted trying to find what can only be found in God. The paths of our choosing will continue to leave us empty and void if they are plans we have made without the direction of God. Also, God will not approve of our good ideas when they move us outside His chosen will for our life.

The difference between a good idea and a God idea is that a God idea will produce peace and it will be fruitful, while a good idea only leads to struggle and confusion. Seek the kingdom of God and His righteousness, and He will lead you into the green pastures He has prepared for you. His plan for your life has already been prepared, so allow Him to guide your steps. Before you move forward, be sure it is a God idea and not just a good one.

www.ingramcontent.com/pod-product-compliance
Lightning Source LLC
Chambersburg PA
CBHW040155160726
48006CB00014B/1760